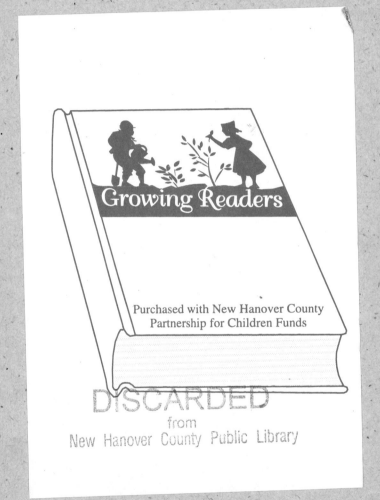

OCEAN DAY

OCEAN DAY

Written by Shelley Rotner and Ken Kreisler
Photographs by Shelley Rotner

MACMILLAN PUBLISHING COMPANY   NEW YORK   MAXWELL MACMILLAN CANADA   TORONTO

MAXWELL MACMILLAN INTERNATIONAL   NEW YORK   OXFORD   SINGAPORE   SYDNEY

10 9 8 7 6 5 4 3 2 1

Library of Congress Cataloging-in-Publication Data
Rotner, Shelley. Ocean day / written by Shelley Rotner and Ken Kreisler ; photographs by Shelley
Rotner. — 1st ed.   p.   cm. Summary: A little girl visits the ocean and discovers many things about
the seashore and the creatures who live there. ISBN 0-02-777886-X   [1. Seashore—Fiction.]
I. Kreisler, Ken. II. Title. PZ7.R752Oc 1993   [E]—dc20   92-6114

For my parents, who have shared their love of the ocean with me. —S.R.

For Rockaway Beach; Stanley, Marcia, Ellen, Linda, Amy;
and Babe and Chelsea, the two best dogs on any beach. —K.K.

Emily loved to go to the ocean—
there were so many things to see.

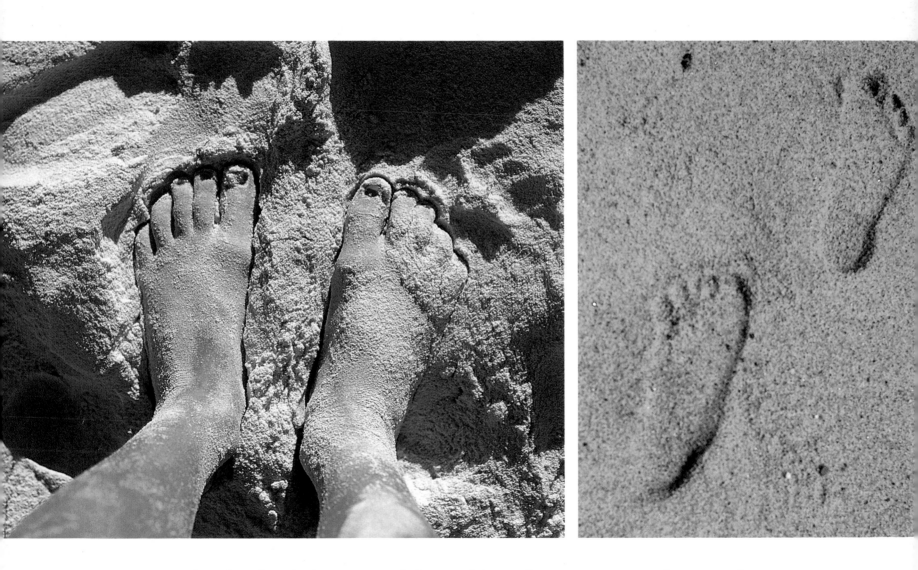

She looked down and found her footprints in the sand,
and danced with her shadow in the sun.

She found a tide pool where many creatures lived.
There were starfish and shiny blue mussels,

sea urchins, snails, and barnacles, too.

A crab scurried to hide.

Emily asked her mom why a fish was lying on the beach.
Her mother said, "Tides come and go. The ocean gives and takes."

Waves make bubbles. Bubbles make foam.
Patterns form in the sand.

Seashells dot the ocean shore—scallop, clam,

moon snail, whelk.

Beach-plum bushes flower.
Driftwood is sculpted by sand and water.

Beach grass, wind, and sand make dunes.
Clouds drift by.

Sunlight shimmers on the water.

Seagulls soar.
Waves crash.

Kites flap.

Children dig and build.

Mothers and fathers call, "It's time to go."
And Emily says, "Good-bye for now."